MOVIE STORYBOOK

 Published in the United States by Random House Children's Books, a division of Penguin Random House LLC, 1745 Broadway, New York, NY 10019, and in Canada by Penguin Random House Canada Limited, Toronto, in conjunction with Disney Enterprises, Inc. Random House and the colophon are registered trademarks of Penguin Random House LLC.
rhcbooks.com
ISBN 978-0-7364-3754-7
Printed in the United States of America
10 9 8 7 6 5 4 3 2 1

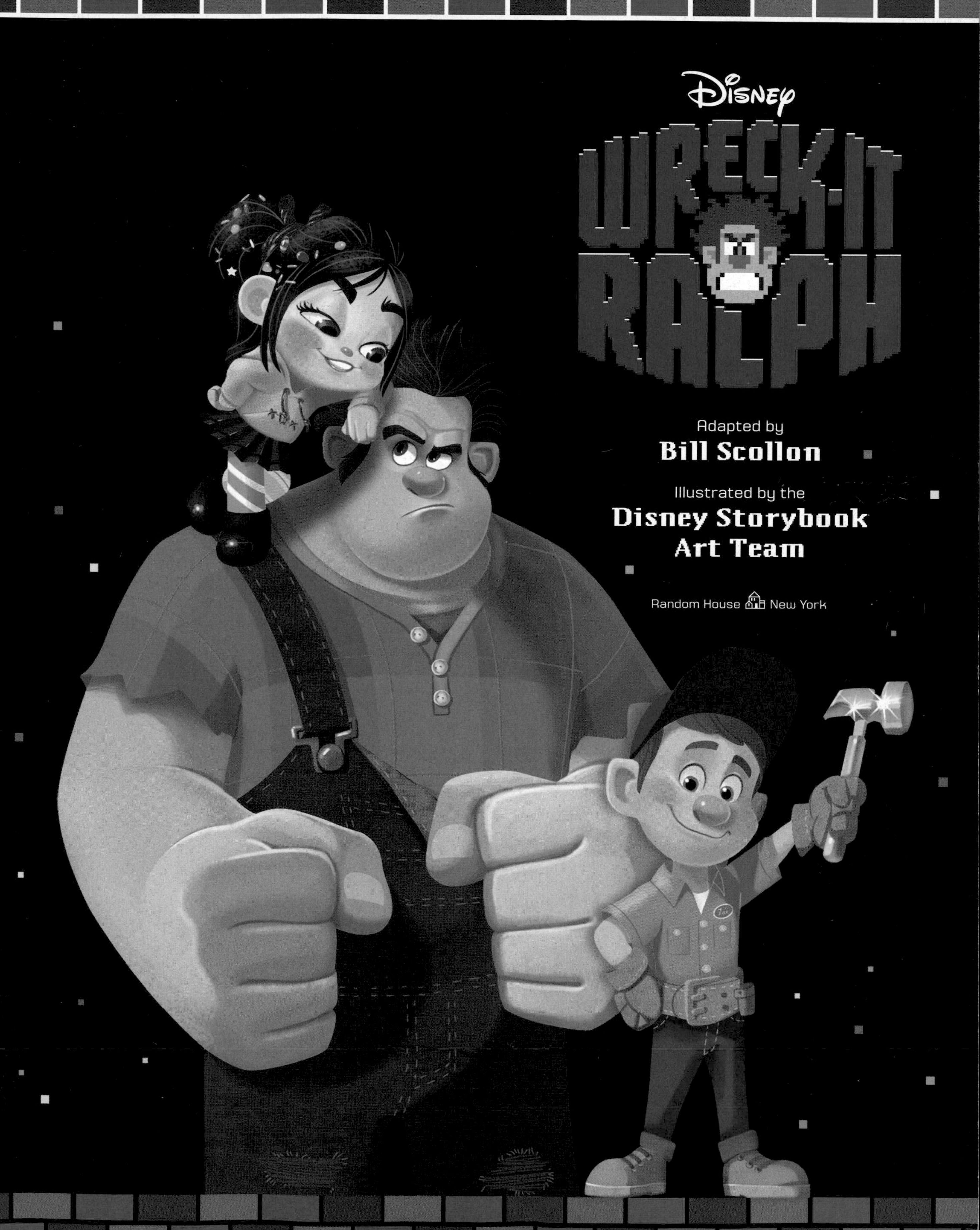

Disney

Wreck-It Ralph

Adapted by
Bill Scollon

Illustrated by the
Disney Storybook Art Team

Random House New York

Wreck-It Ralph worked hard as the Bad Guy in the *Fix-It Felix Jr.* arcade game. Every time someone dropped a coin in the game, Ralph appeared and yelled, **"I'M GONNA WRECK IT!"**

Then he'd smash the apartment building in Niceland to pieces! When he was done, Fix-It Felix, the **Good Guy**, would arrive with his magic **hammer** and fix everything Ralph had wrecked. The Nicelanders always cheered for Felix. They even gave him a medal and a pie!

But they never cheered for Ralph. Instead, they **threw him** off the building. . . .

SPLAT! Ralph landed in a mud puddle.

The old 8-bit video game had stood in Litwak's Family Fun Center and Arcade for thirty years. But *inside* the game, Ralph had grown **tired** of being thrown in the mud while Felix won pies and medals. It didn't seem fair.

Why couldn't *he* be the **Good Guy** once in a while?

One night, Ralph took a trip through the power cord to attend a meeting of Bad-Anon, a **support group** for video-game Bad Guys.

Ralph admitted to the group that he wished he could be the Good Guy for a change.

The Bad Guys were **horrified**. You can't change who you are, they insisted. But Ralph was not convinced.

When Ralph returned home, the Nicelanders were having a **party** to celebrate the game's thirtieth anniversary. But they hadn't even bothered to invite Ralph! That didn't sit well with him. **"I'm going to that party!"** he grumbled.

The party was in full swing when Ralph entered the penthouse . . . and spotted the cake. He couldn't believe his eyes. There was a mini figure of Felix wearing his medal on top of the cake. Why wasn't there a mini figure of Ralph wearing a medal, too?

One of the Nicelanders scoffed. **"Bad Guys don't win medals."** Ralph was so upset that he smashed the cake!

Ralph felt awful. He left the party and went to a restaurant for a root beer. At the bar, he met a soldier from the ***Hero's Duty*** game. Ralph learned that the goal of that game was to defeat cy-bugs and climb a tower to get the Medal of Heroes.

All of a sudden, an ordinary bug skittered across the counter. The traumatized soldier **freaked out** at the sight of it!

Ralph quickly came up with a plan. He borrowed the soldier's armor and snuck into *Hero's Duty* to look for the medal. When the game started, huge cy-bugs swooped down—and attacked! They devoured everything in their path.

Ralph ran for his life!

Ralph made a mess, which caused the game to stop. **GAME OVER!** As the game began to reset, a bright light drew the cy-bugs to the tower and zapped them!

The leader of the soldiers, **Sergeant Calhoun**, yelled at Ralph.

She was angry at him for not following her orders.

But Ralph wasn't paying attention. He was trying to figure out a way to get up the tower and take the **Medal of Heroes** for himself!

Meanwhile, a player in Litwak's put some coins into the *Fix-It Felix Jr.* game. She was ready to play! But Felix had nothing to fix. There was no one to wreck the building!

"This game is busted," the girl told Mr. Litwak.

Mr. Litwak slapped an **Out of Order** sign on the game. Inside, the Nicelanders were shocked. What would they do if Mr. Litwak unplugged it? Where would they go?

Luckily, Felix had found out where Ralph had gone. He was ready to bring Ralph back home. "I can fix this!" he said.

Back in *Hero's Duty*, Ralph had climbed the tower and could almost reach the medal. All he had to do was sneak past dozens of cy-bug eggs without touching them. Amazingly, **he did it**!

But as Ralph tried to make his escape with the medal, he accidentally knocked over an egg. A baby cy-bug flew out and landed on his face. Ralph staggered backward, fell into an escape pod, and **blasted off**!

Just then, Felix entered *Hero's Duty*. He and Sergeant Calhoun spotted Ralph's escape pod as it **zoomed** out of the game!

The escape pod crash-landed in **SUGAR RUSH**, a go-kart racing game set in a world made entirely of candy.

The cy-bug fell into a chocolate pond and ***DISAPPEARED***.

Ralph thought he'd lost his medal in the crash, but he spotted it hanging from a peppermint tree. Suddenly, a little girl named Vanellope von Schweetz appeared. To her, the medal looked like a gold coin. ***"RACE YOU FOR IT!"*** she yelled.

Ralph tried to climb the peppermint tree, but he fell into a pool of sticky taffy!

Vanellope took the medal to ***SUGAR RUSH STADIUM***, where a race was about to begin. King Candy announced that every racer needed a coin to enter. Vanellope pushed her kart out of the shadows and tossed Ralph's medal into the pot.

It worked! Vanellope's name appeared on the list of racers. King Candy and the rest of the crowd **GASPED**.

To them, Vanellope was nothing more than a troublesome glitch, a mistake in the game's programming.

"STOP HER!" shouted the king.

Suddenly, Ralph ran onto the track. He was covered in taffy! Ralph only wanted to get his medal back, but the crowd thought he was a ***CANDY MONSTER***!

8

Ralph was taken into custody by the Donut Police, but he quickly escaped. He tracked Vanellope to the Lollistix Forest. There, a group of racers confronted Vanellope and demanded that she drop out of the race. When she told them to forget it, they ***SMASHED*** her kart and ***PUSHED*** her into the mud!

THAT MADE RALPH MAD! He chased the mean racers away. Vanellope was grateful, so she promised to give Ralph his medal back . . . if she won the race. But first she needed a new kart. **RALPH GRUDGINGLY AGREED TO HELP.**

Meanwhile, Felix and Calhoun followed Ralph into *Sugar Rush*. They found his wrecked escape pod, but there was no sign of him or the cy-bug. Felix was afraid Ralph might have **GONE TURBO**.

Felix explained that years before, Turbo had been the **STAR** of a **POPULAR** racing game.

But when a new game arrived in the arcade, Turbo had abandoned his own game and tried to take over the new one.

When the players saw the old Turbo in the new game, they thought it was **MALFUNCTIONING**. The new game was **UNPLUGGED** and **HAULED AWAY**.

"If I don't fix this mess," said Felix, "the same thing's going to happen to *my* game."

START
SUGAR
MILK
FLOUR

Meanwhile, Vanellope had taken Ralph to the *Sugar Rush* kart bakery. They tried to bake a new kart, but Ralph wrecked some of the equipment. The kart that came out was a crazy, mixed-up mess.

VANELLOPE LOVED IT!

Unfortunately, King Candy found them. Vanellope hopped into her new kart and drove Ralph to a secret mountain where she had been living—right next to a lake of hot diet cola with stalactites of Mentos candy hanging over it.

Ralph created a practice track so Vanellope could perfect her driving skills. She was soon speeding along, but she couldn't stop **GLITCHING**!

GLITCH

King Candy secretly pulled Ralph aside when Vanellope took a break. He told Ralph that Vanellope was in **DANGER**. If players in the arcade saw her glitching, they'd think *Sugar Rush* was **BROKEN** and the game would be **UNPLUGGED**.

The king gave Ralph his medal back and asked him to stop Vanellope from racing. He swore it was the only way to protect her.

Just after King Candy made his exit, Vanellope surprised Ralph with a new medal she'd made especially for him. One side read "To Stink Brain." The other said ***"YOU'RE MY HERO!"***

When Vanellope saw Ralph's medal in his pocket, she was angry. Ralph tried to explain to her what King Candy had said, but Vanellope wouldn't listen. She would never agree to give up her dream of racing! Desperate to protect her, Ralph ***WRECKED*** Vanellope's kart!

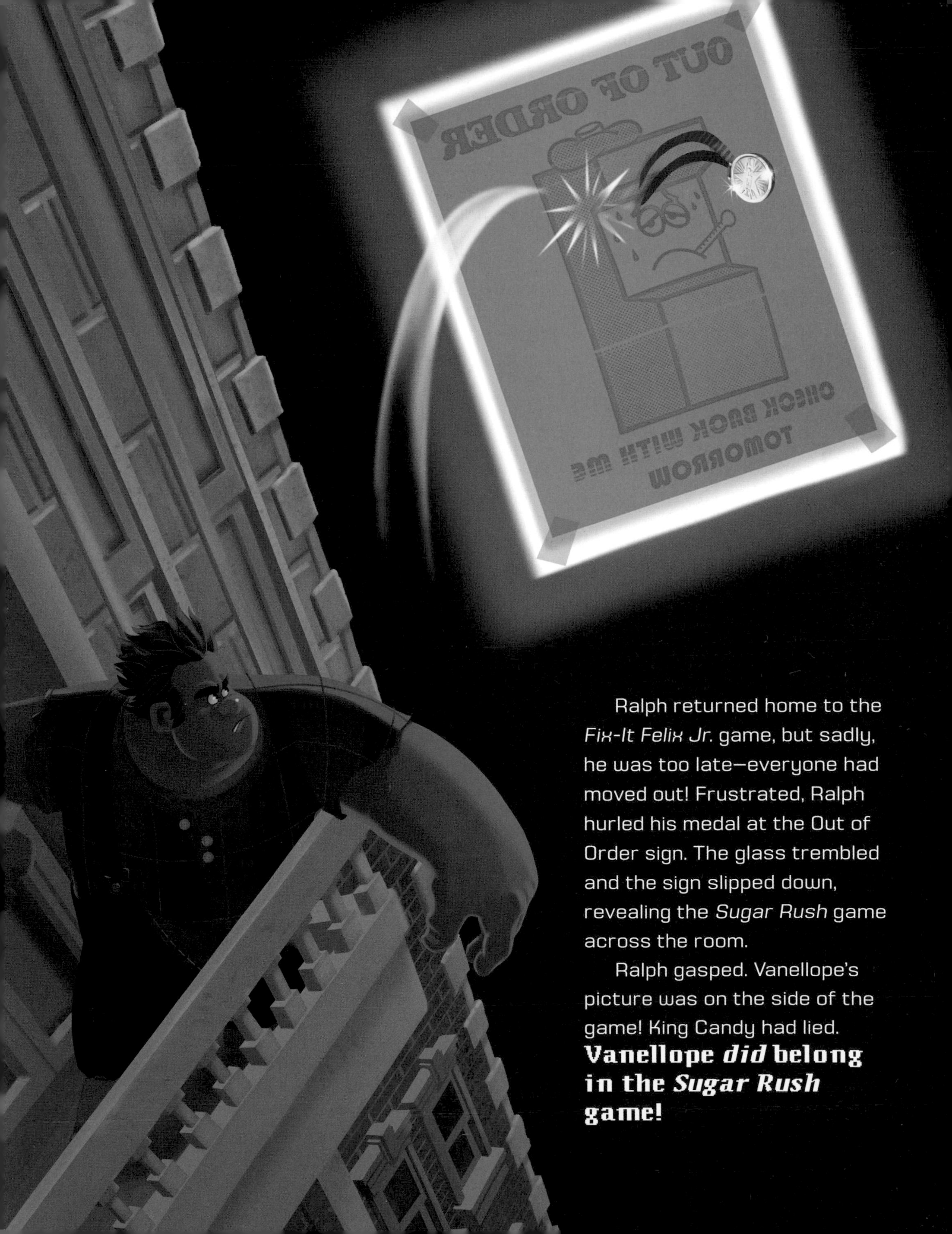

Ralph returned home to the *Fix-It Felix Jr.* game, but sadly, he was too late—everyone had moved out! Frustrated, Ralph hurled his medal at the Out of Order sign. The glass trembled and the sign slipped down, revealing the *Sugar Rush* game across the room.

Ralph gasped. Vanellope's picture was on the side of the game! King Candy had lied. **Vanellope *did* belong in the *Sugar Rush* game!**

Ralph hurried back to *Sugar Rush* and found Felix locked in King Candy's dungeon! Ralph **BROKE DOWN** the walls and asked Felix for help.

Felix agreed to **FIX** Vanellope's kart right away!

Ralph, Felix, and Vanellope rushed to the stadium, where the race had already begun. Vanellope hopped into her kart and joined in! She quickly caught up to the other racers—***GLITCHING*** and ***TWITCHING*** along the way—and pulled up next to King Candy.

King Candy slammed into Vanellope's kart and started to glitch, too! As everyone watched on the big screen, the king flickered and transformed into ***TURBO***!

"YOU RUINED EVERYTHING!" he yelled just before changing back to King Candy.

Vanellope was on her way to winning the race! But cy-bugs suddenly burst out of the ground! Before long, the cy-bugs had ***DESTROYED*** the finish line. Ralph was able to rescue Vanellope, but King Candy was ***GOBBLED UP*** by the nasty creatures!

Ralph knew a bright light would draw the cy-bugs away, so he rushed to the top of Diet Cola Mountain. There he was attacked by the newly transformed **KING CANDY CY-BUG**!

Ralph knew what he had to do. He smashed through the ceiling of Diet Cola Mountain. Soon the Mentos stalactites started to break free. With no time to spare, Vanellope glitched through the wall and saved Ralph from falling into the bubbling cola!

When the Mentos hit the cola, a glowing ***GEYSER*** shot out of the top of the mountain. The cy-bugs were helpless as they flew to the light. ***ZAP! ZAP!***

With the cy-bugs gone, Felix fixed the finish line. Ralph cautiously **PUSHED** Vanellope across. Happily, the game did not shut down. Instead, something wonderful happened. . . .

Vanellope turned into a **PRINCESS**! She finally had her true identity back!

YTA
BING!
24
capacity
RA

Vanellope gave Ralph a big hug. She wanted him to stay with her in *Sugar Rush*. "You could be happy," she told him.

Ralph smiled. "I'm already happy, because I have the **COOLEST FRIEND** in the world."

Back in the arcade, Mr. Litwak was seconds away from unplugging the *Fix-It Felix Jr.* game. But a little girl shouted with excitement. The game was working again!

Ralph had come home.

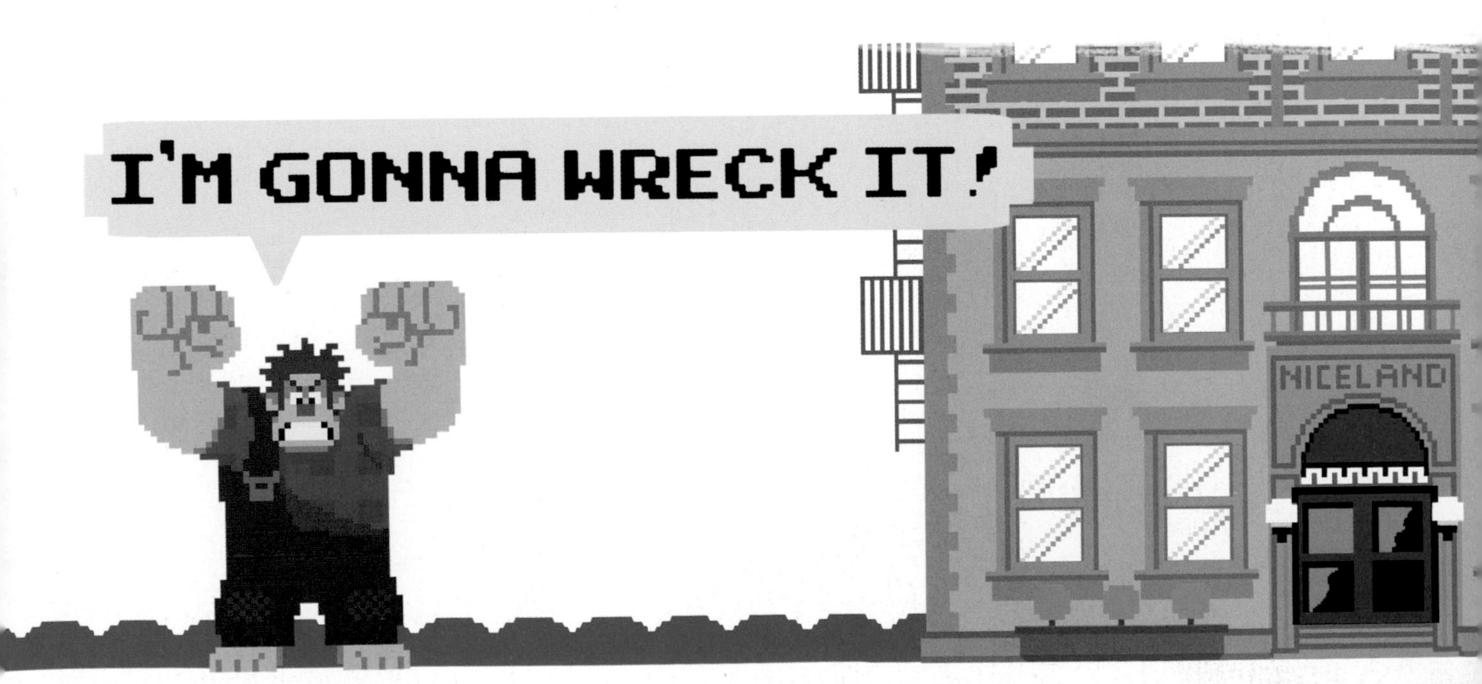

The Nicelanders gave Ralph a cake. He was happy to be the **Bad Guy** again. After all, with a friend as nice as Vanellope, how bad could he really be?

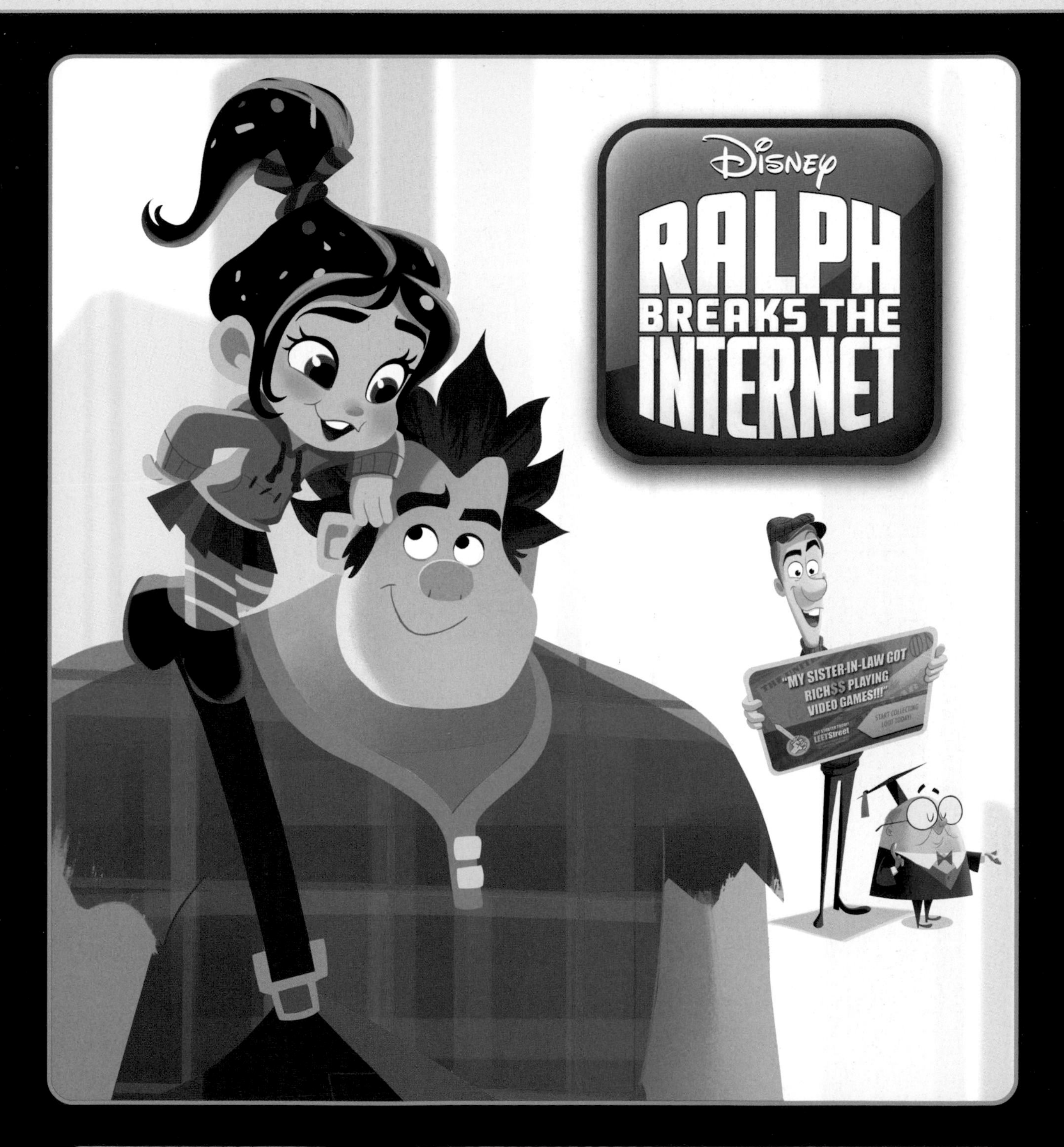

Adapted by
Bill Scollon

Illustrated by the
Disney Storybook Art Team

Wreck-It Ralph and Vanellope von Schweetz were best friends. Ralph was the Bad Guy in the popular game *Fix-It Felix Jr*, and Vanellope was the best racer in *Sugar Rush*.

They did everything together!

Every day before the sun came up in Litwak's Family Fun Center and Arcade, they met in Game Central Station, which was located in the power strip. One day, Mr. Litwak plugged in something new and different—a Wi-Fi router!

Vanellope thought doing something different sounded good. She knew every turn and obstacle in *Sugar Rush* by heart. Even though she loved it, the race **wasn't much of a challenge** anymore.

That gave Ralph an idea. He hurried into the game ahead of Vanellope and pounded out a new off-road track.

Vanellope loved it, but Swati, the game's player, thought something was wrong.

Swati turned Vanellope's steering wheel so hard, it **broke** off!

Mr. Litwak tried to put the steering wheel back on, but it **snapped in two**. He said he couldn't order a new one. The company that made *Sugar Rush* had gone **out of business**.

Swati found a used steering wheel on eBay. But Mr. Litwak said it was too expensive. Sadly, it was time to **retire *Sugar Rush***.

"Litwak's going to **unplug** your game!" shouted Ralph.

All the *Sugar Rush* characters ran out the exit and into Game Central Station. Fix-It Felix arranged for them to stay in the Nicelander apartment building.

The residents took everyone in—**except** the game's high-spirited racers. Finally, Sergeant Calhoun, Felix's wife, stepped forward and volunteered to take them all! **Surge Protector tried to warn the two** about overloading their home, but they wouldn't listen.

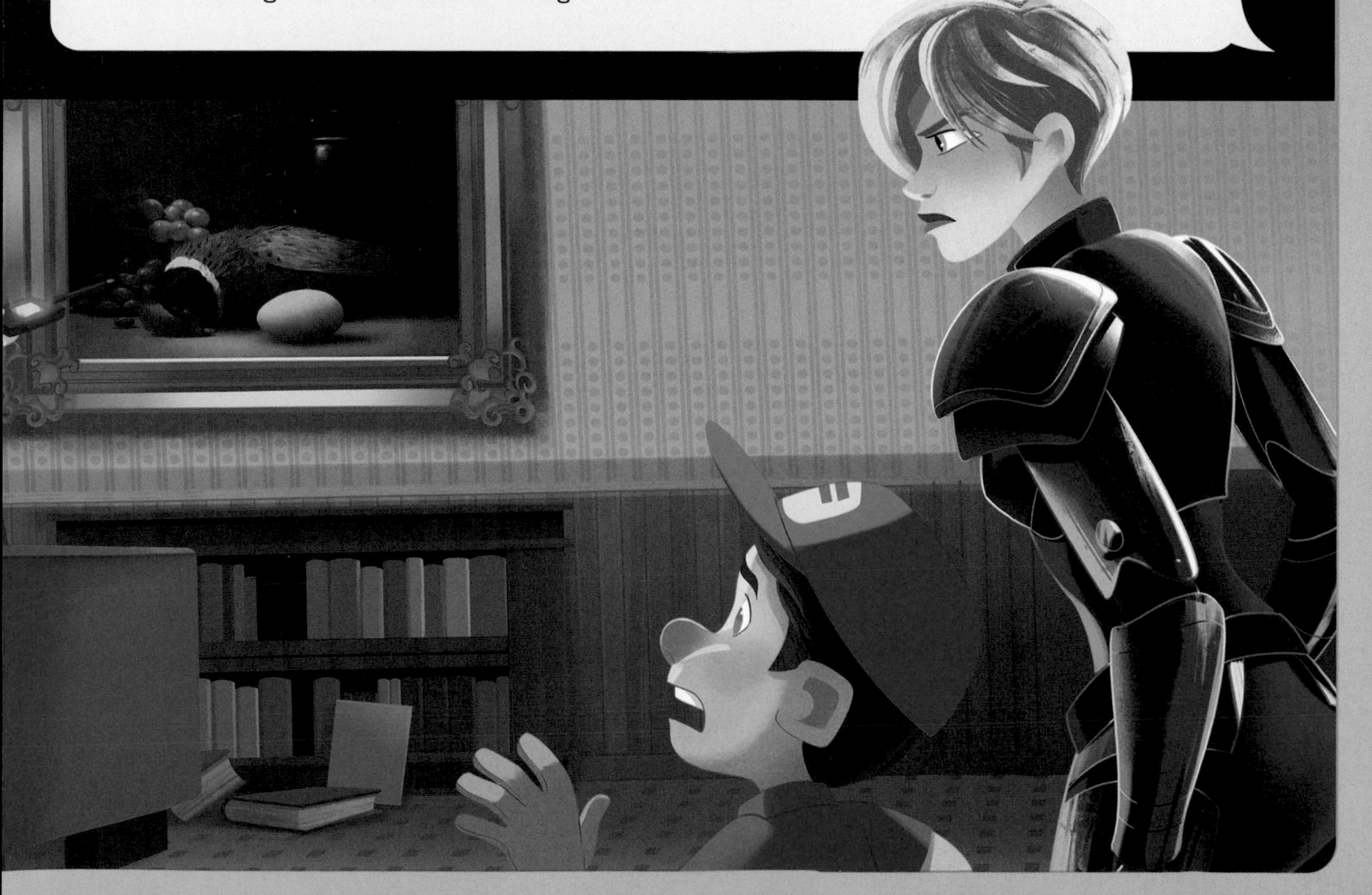

Later that day, Ralph and Felix were feeling **gloomy** about what had happened to *Sugar Rush*. Ralph wondered if it was all his fault. But he perked up when he remembered the steering wheel Swati had found on eBay. Getting it meant Vanellope would be able to return to her game and the racers would leave Felix's apartment!

Ralph hurried off to find Vanellope—he couldn't wait to tell her the good news!

"Vanellope, we're going to the **Internet**. Come on!"

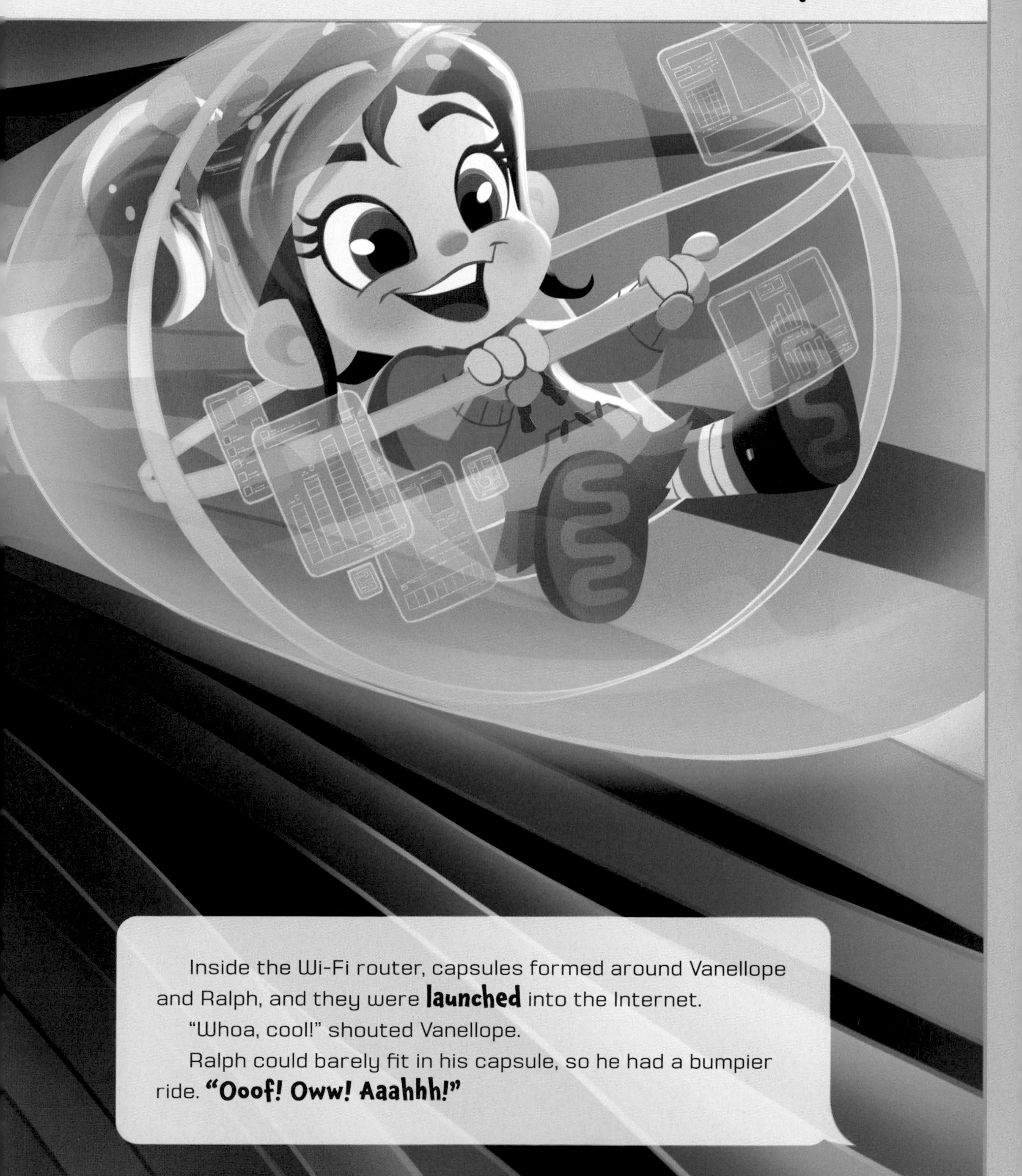

Inside the Wi-Fi router, capsules formed around Vanellope and Ralph, and they were **launched** into the Internet.

"Whoa, cool!" shouted Vanellope.

Ralph could barely fit in his capsule, so he had a bumpier ride. **"Ooof! Oww! Aaahhh!"**

"Sweet mother of monkey milk!" exclaimed Vanellope. The world of the Internet was so big, they had no idea how they'd ever find the place called eBay.

KnowsMore had the answer. In fact, he had *all* the answers. KnowsMore ran a search bar. As soon as he knew what to look for, he found the steering wheel in milliseconds.

Vanellope and Ralph were quickly **whisked away**!

"We're gonna do it, Ralph. We're actually gonna **save** my game."

"Told ya not to worry. We just gotta keep our eyes on the **prize**."

When they got to eBay, there was a group of **pop-up ads** outside. They offered a variety of items that you could get with just **one click**. But Ralph and Vanellope were in a hurry, so they continued.

Inside eBay, the auction for the *Sugar Rush* steering wheel had already begun. A bidder shouted out a **number**.

Vanellope had a hunch. "I think all you have to do is yell out the biggest number and you win," she said. Before long, the number got so high that the other bidder dropped out—leaving only Ralph and Vanellope!

"Sold!" shouted the auctioneer. "For twenty-seven thousand and one!"

At the checkout, Ralph and Vanellope learned they had to pay **$27,001**! And if they didn't pay in twenty-four hours, they'd lose the bid.

Ralph remembered a fellow named **Spamley** who'd had a pop-up ad claiming that people could get rich playing video games.

Ralph and Vanellope went to his website. Spamley and his partner, Gord, showed them a list of items from games that would earn them money. One was a fast car from *Slaughter Race* that was worth much more than they needed.

The car belonged to **Shank, the game's fastest and toughest racer**. Ralph and Vanellope watched as two other players tried to steal Shank's car. Shank and her crew easily knocked them out of the game.

HOT MAMA

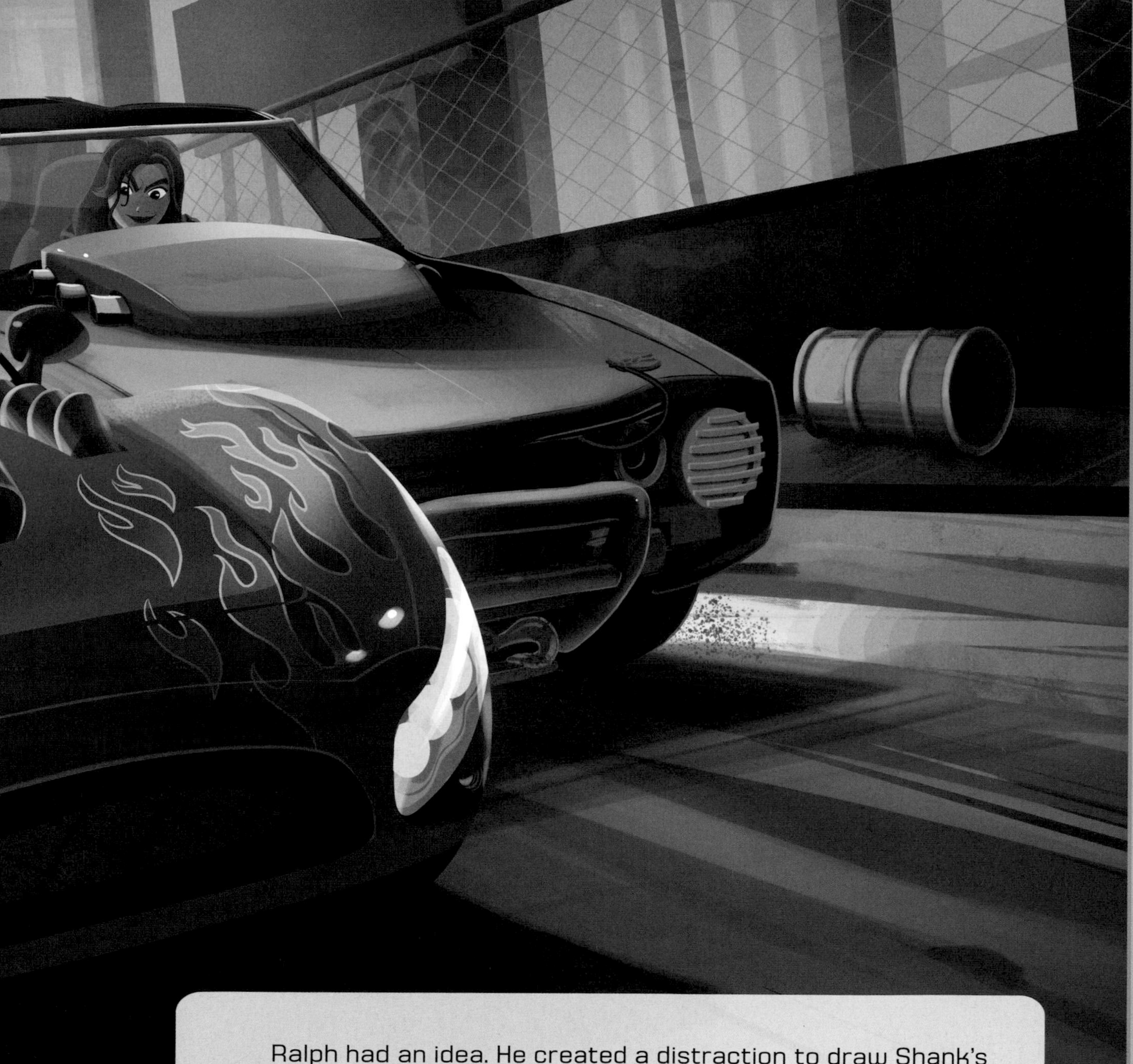

Ralph had an idea. He created a distraction to draw Shank's attention away from the car.

Vanellope jumped behind the wheel and stepped on the gas. **They had Shank's race car!**

But Shank was not going to give up that easily—she hopped into another car and quickly caught up to Ralph and Vanellope!

Vanellope did her best, but the *Sugar Rush* racer couldn't outrace Shank. **She lost.**

Ralph tried to explain. He told Shank they needed her car so they could earn enough money to save Vanellope's racing game.

Surprisingly, Shank wanted to help, and she knew just what to do. She had one of the members of her crew **blast Ralph with a leaf blower**. Another recorded it on her phone! Shank said her friend Yesss could help them make money by putting **crazy videos** like that on the Internet.

ENTER AT YOUR OWN

Just outside *Slaughter Race*, Vanellope bounced with excitement. She loved the racing game, and she was also very fond of Shank.

"She looks cool. She drives cool. Her car is cool."

But Ralph didn't trust Shank.

Suddenly, a messenger popped up to let them know that their eBay bid would expire in eight hours.

Vanellope tried to convice Ralph that going to Yesss at BuzzzTube was the fastest way for them to make money. Reluctantly, Ralph agreed.

Yesss ran the **insanely popular** video-sharing site BuzzzTube. She loved Ralph's video.

When Yesss checked the video online, she was amazed at how many hearts it had received from viewers.

"The hearts are money," Yesss explained.

"We already have **forty-three dollars**?"

"Mm-hmm. I predict this video is gonna be huge. I can see the headline now: **Ralph Breaks the Internet**."

FRAGILE

To help Ralph get more hearts, Vanellope volunteered to be part of BuzzzTube's army of pop-up ads. Yesss's limo dropped her off at a popular website called OhMyDisney.com.

But Vanellope was an **unauthorized pop-up**, so she had to hide to avoid being caught. She glitched through a locked door and found herself face to face with avatars of the Disney princesses!

Vanellope told them she was a princess, too—the **Princess of Sugar Rush**—and everyone became fast friends. Soon all the princesses were sporting a more casual look, like Vanellope!

Meanwhile, time was running out. Even though Ralph and Yesss had been busy making funny videos, they needed **one more** to make enough money to buy the steering wheel.

While Yesss tried to upload a new video, Ralph headed down to the main floor of BuzzzTube to get more hearts. He ended up in a room full of comments. He'd thought everyone on the Internet loved him, but he soon learned he was wrong. Some people hated him!

Regardless of how those people felt, the latest video was a hit! Now Ralph and Vanellope had **more than enough money**!

ch sad. so disappoint
1s ago
REPLY
ate everything about this.
1s ago
22
2
REPLY
@ClickClickClick
y iz he gamez?
2s ago
1
20
REPLY
@FanFace
loser vibe is strong.
1s ago
3
0
REPLY
guh. wut gar-baj
1s ago
10
5
REPLY
2s ago
6
4
REPLY
all the heartz
1s ago
5
4
REPLY
this is the premium content i came for
1s ago
7
REPLY
@JuniperBan
3s ago
30
2
REPLY
blech.
1s ago
lrn2internet
do. not. want. like ever.
@lophatmcgoo
blech.
1s ago
15
9
REPLY
do. not. want. like ever.
2s ago
9
1
REPLY
i need an adult right now

SEQUOIA
SPEEDWAY

Ralph paid for the steering wheel and called Vanellope on his phone with an app called **BuzzzyFace**. Without Vanellope realizing it, her phone vibrated off the dashboard and the call was answered. Ralph overheard her tell Shank that she loved *Slaughter Race* so much, **she wasn't going back** to Game Central Station with Ralph.

Ralph felt like his best friend was betraying him.

Gord said his cousin, a **shady character** named Double Dan, had created a virus that would slow down *Slaughter Race*. Hopefully that would make Vanellope lose interest in the game.

Double Dan picked up an exotic wooden box. "Allow me to introduce you to Arthur."

Double Dan explained that Arthur was an insecurity virus. It would find the flaws in *Slaughter Race* and duplicate them. As long as Ralph didn't let the virus escape the game and go into the Internet, no one would get hurt.

Ralph sneaked into *Slaughter Race* and let Arthur loose. Once the virus was **free**, it went to work. But instead of slowing down the game, it scanned everything, looking for weaknesses. When Vanellope glitched, the virus copied the error and spread it through the game!

Walls, buildings, and other race cars glitched, too. *Slaughter Race* started to break apart. The game was **crashing**! A building collapsed on top of Vanellope's car, knocking her out.

SCANNING

SCANNING

SCANNING

INSECURITY DETECTED

Suddenly, the outside of *Slaughter Race* started to shimmer and glitch. Ralph knew something was going wrong inside. "I've got to get her out of there!" he said.

Slaughter Race's firewall was closing! Ralph busted a hole to get in. He had no idea that the virus was able to escape into the Internet through the hole he had made.

Vanellope blamed herself for crashing *Slaughter Race*. "It was my glitch's fault," she said.

"No, it wasn't," Ralph admitted. He told her about the virus and how it was only supposed to slow the game down.

Vanellope was **angry**. She threw Ralph's medal into the Older Net. "You will not follow me!" she declared.

Feeling helpless, Ralph watched her go. He didn't realize that the virus was now scanning *him*.

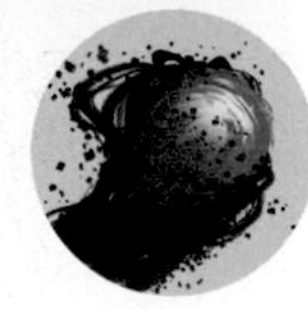

Insecurity detected.

Down in the Older Net, Ralph searched for his medal. But when he found it, it was broken in half. Meanwhile, the virus, fueled by Ralph's insecurities, was cloning itself at a **furious** pace. Millions of Ralph clones were **wrecking** the Internet! Ralph knew he had to save Vanellope.

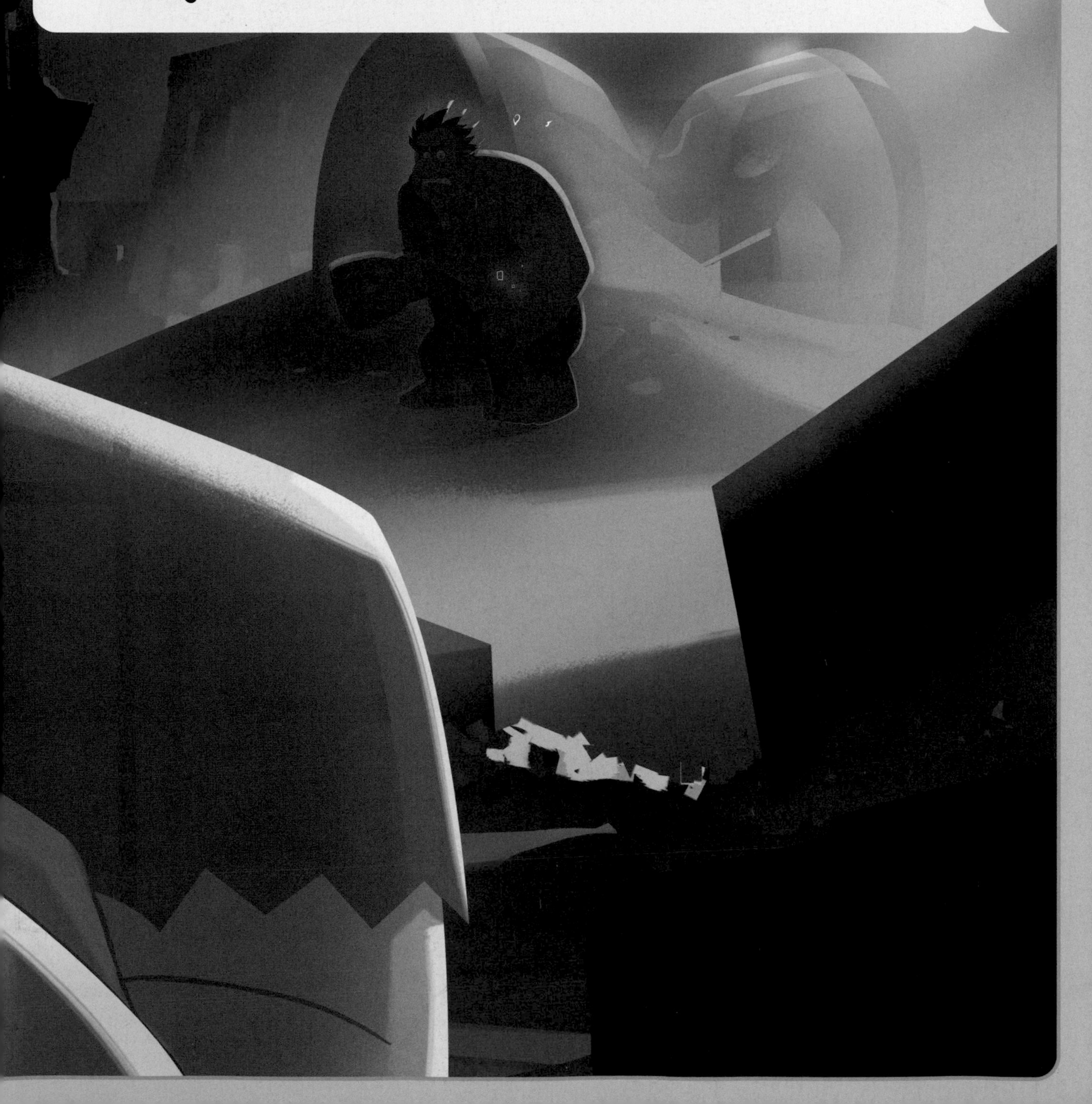

Meanwhile, Vanellope had made her way to KnowsMore, who told her about a section of the Internet that could get rid of the clones. That was when the real Ralph showed up.

Vanellope hatched a plan. Against Ralph's better judgment, Vanellope decided she could use herself as bait to lure the clones into the Anti-Virus District. Then *Slaughter Race*—and the Internet—would be saved! All they needed was a car.

Yesss zoomed up in her limo, and Vanellope and Ralph got in. Vanellope taunted the clones: "It's me, your bestest friend in the whole wide world." It worked! **"Woo-hoo!"**

Unfortunately, the clones caused the limo to crash. Everyone was okay—but not for long.

Millions of clones came together and formed one **gigantic Ralph**! It grabbed Vanellope and climbed to the top of a skyscraper. Ralph tried to save her, but he was caught, too! Gigantic Ralph began to squeeze him.

"Stop it!" Vanellope yelled. "Take me! Just put him down. I'll be your **only friend**," she told the giant Ralph.

"No! You don't own her. That's **not** how friendship works," the real Ralph explained. "You need to let her go." He turned to Vanellope. "And we're gonna be okay, right, kid?"

"Always," she answered. Suddenly, the clones began to **dissolve** as Ralph's insecurity disappeared. The Internet was saved!